THE WOLF OF GOD.

CLASSIC FANTASY AND HORROR

GOLU KUMAR

Contents

1. Chapter 1 1

ONE

I.

As the little steamer entered the bay of Kettletoft in the Orkneys the beach at Sanday appeared so low that the houses almost seemed to be standing in the water; and to the big, dark man leaning over the rail of the upper deck the sight of them came with a pang of mingled pain and pleasure. The scene, to his eyes, had not changed. The houses, the low shore, the flat treeless country beyond, and the vast open sky, all looked the same as when he left the island thirty years ago to work for the Hudson Bay Company in distant N. W. Canada. A lad of eighteen then, he was now a man of forty-eight, old for his years, and this was the homecoming he had so often dreamed about in the lonely wilderness of trees where he had spent his life. Yet his grim face wore an anxious rather than a tender expression. The return was perhaps not quite as he had pictured it.

As the little steamer entered the bay of Kettletoft in the Orkneys the beach at Sanday appeared so low that the houses almost seemed to be standing in the water; and to the big, dark man leaning over the rail of the upper deck the sight of them came with a pang of mingled pain and pleasure. The scene, to his eyes, had not changed. The houses, the low shore, the flat treeless country beyond, and the vast open sky, all looked the same as when he left the island thirty years ago to work for the Hudson Bay Company in distant N. W. Canada. A lad of eighteen then, he was now a man of forty-eight, old for his years, and this was the homecoming he had so often dreamed about in the lonely wilderness of trees where he had spent his life. Yet his grim face wore an anxious rather than a tender expression. The return was perhaps not quite as he had pictured it.

A curious expression now flickered over his weather-hardened face as he saw again his childhood's home, and then return, so often dreamed about, actually took place at last. An uneasy light flashed for a moment in the deep-set grey eyes but was quickly gone again, and the tanned visage recovered its accustomed look of stern composure. His keen sight took in a dark knot of figures on the landing pier--his brother, he knew, among them. A wave of homesickness swept over him. He longed to see his brother again, the old farm, the sweep of open country, the dunes, and the breaking seas. The smell of long-forgotten days came to his nostrils with its sweet, painful pang of youthful memories.

How fine, he thought, to be back there in the old familiar fields of childhood, with sea and sand about him instead of the smother of endless woods that ran a thousand miles without a break. He was glad in particular that no trees were visible, and that rabbits scampering among the dunes were the only wild animals he need ever meet...

Those thirty years in the woods, it seemed, oppressed his mind; the forests, the countless multitudes of trees, had wearied him. His nerves, perhaps, had suffered finally. Snow, frost and sun, stars, and the wind had been his companions during the long days and endless nights in his lonely Post, but chiefly--trees. Trees, trees, trees! On the whole, he had preferred them in stormy weather, though, in another way, their rigid hosts, 'mid the deep silence of still days, had been equally oppressive. In the clear sunlight of a windless day, they assumed a waiting, listening, watching aspect that had something spectral in it, but when in motion--well, he preferred a moving animal to one that stood stock-still and stared. Wind, moreover, in a million trees, even the lightest breeze, drowned all other sounds--the howling of the wolves, for instance, in winter, or the ceaseless harsh barking of the husky dogs he so disliked.

Even on this warm September afternoon, a slight shiver ran over him as the background of dead years loomed up behind the present scene. He thrust the picture back, deep down inside himself. The self-control, the strong, even violent will that the face betrayed, came into operation instantly. The background was background; it belonged to what was past, and the past was over and done with. It was dead. Jim meant it to stay dead.

The figure waving to him from the pier was his brother. He knew Tom instantly; the years had dealt easily with him on this quiet island; there was no startling, no unkindly change, and deep emotion, though unexpressed, rose in his heart. It was good to be home again, he realized, as he sat presently in the cart, Tom holding the reins, driving slowly back to the farm at the north end of the island. Everything he found familiar, yet at the same time strange. They passed the school where he used to go as a little bare-legged boy; other boys were now learning their lessons exactly as he used to do. Through the open window, he could hear the droning voice of the schoolmaster, who, though invisible, wore the face of Mr. Lovibond, his teacher.

"Lovibond?" said Tom, in reply to his question. "Oh, he's been dead these twenty years. He went south, you know--

Glasgow, I think it was, or Edinburgh. He got typhoid."

Stands of golden plover were to be seen as of old in the fields, or flashing overhead in swift flight with a whir of wings, wheeling and turning together like one huge bird. Down on the empty shore, a curlew cried. Its piercing note rose clear above the noisy clamor of the gulls. The sun played softly on the quiet sea, the air was keen but pleasant, the tang of salt mixed sweetly with the clean smells of open country that he knew so well. Nothing of essentials had changed, even the low clouds beyond the heaving uplands were the clouds of childhood.

They soon arrived at the dunes, where rabbits were either sitting at the mouths of their burrows or running erratically across the road in front of the sluggish cart.

They are secure until the colder weather arrives and trapping starts, he said. He recalled every detail in great detail.

Tom retorted, "And they know it, too—the cunning little beggars." He inquired idly, "Any rabbits out where you've been?"

His brother quickly responded, "Not to injure you.

Nothing seemed to change, although everything seemed different. He looked upon the old, familiar things, but with other eyes. There were, of course, changes, alterations, yet so slight, in a way so odd and curious, that they evaded him; not being of the physical order, they reported to his soul, not to his mind. But his soul, being troubled, sought to deny the changes; to admit them meant to admit a change in himself he had determined to conceal even if he could not entirely deny it.

"Same old place, Tom," came one of his rare remarks. "The years ain't done much to it." He looked into his brother's face a moment squarely. "Nor do you, either, Tom," he added, affection and tenderness just touching his voice and breaking through a natural reserve that was almost taciturnity.

His brother returned the look; and something in that instant passed between the two men, something of understanding that no words had hinted at, much less expressed. The tie was real, they loved each other, they were loyal, true, steadfast fellows. In youth, they had known no secrets. The shadow that now passed and vanished left vague trouble in both hearts.

"Jim, the forests have turned you into a mute man, replied Tom softly.

I imagine you'll miss them around here."

The curt response was, "Maybe, but I guess not,"

His lips snapped as though they were of steel and could never open again, while the tone he used made Tom realize that the subject was not one his brother cared to talk about particularly. He was surprised, therefore, when, after a pause, Jim returned to it of his own accord. He was sitting a little sideways as he spoke, taking in the scene with hungry eyes. "It's a queer thing," he observed, "to look round and see nothing but clean empty land, and not a single tree in sight. You see, it doesn't look natural quiet."

Again his brother was struck by the tone of voice, but this time by something else as well he could not name. Jim was excusing himself, explaining. The manner, too, arrested him. And thirty years disappeared as though they had not been, for it was thus Jim acted as a boy when there was something unpleasant he had to say and wished to get it over. The tone, the gesture, the manner, all were there. He was edging up to something he wished to say, yet dared not utter.

"You've had enough of trees then?" Tom said sympathetically, trying to help, "and things?"

The instant the last two words were out he realized that they had been drawn from him instinctively and that it was the anxiety of deep affection which had prompted them. He had guessed without knowing he had guessed, or rather, without intention or attempt to guess. Jim had a secret. Love's clairvoyance had discovered it, though not yet its hidden terms.

"I have----" began the other, then paused, evidently to choose his words with care. "I've had enough of trees." He was about to speak of something that his brother had unwittingly touched upon in his chance phrase, but instead of finding the words he sought, he gave a sudden start, his breath caught sharply. "What's that?" he exclaimed, jerking his body around so abruptly that Tom automatically pulled the reins. "What is it?"

"A dog barking," Tom answered, much surprised. "A farm dog barking. Why? What did you think it was?" he asked, as he flicked the horse to go on again. "You made me jump," he added, with a laugh. "You're used to huskies, ain't you?"

"It sounded so--not like a dog, I mean," came the slow explanation. "It's long since I heard a sheep-dog bark, I suppose it startled me."

"Oh, it's a dog all right," Tom assured him comfortingly, for his heart told him infallibly the kind of tone to use. And presently, too, he changed the subject in his blunt, honest fashion, knowing that, also, was the right and kindly thing to do. He pointed out the old farms as they drove along, his brother silent again, sitting stiff and rigid at his side. "And it's good to have you back, Jim, from those outlandish places. There are not too many of the family left now--just you and I."

"Just you and I," the other repeated gruffly, but in a sweetened tone that proved he appreciated the ready sympathy and tact. "We'll stick together, Tom, eh? Blood's thicker than water, ain't it? I've learned that much, anyhow."

The voice had something gentle and appealing in it, something his brother heard now for the first time. An elbow nudged into his side, and Tom knew the gesture was not solely a sign of affection but grew partly also from the comfort born of physical contact when the heart is anxious. The touch, like the last words, conveyed an appeal for help. Tom was so surprised he couldn't believe it quite.

Scared! Jim scared! The thought puzzled and afflicted him who knew his brother's character inside out, his courage, his presence of mind in danger, his resolution. Jim frightened seemed an impossibility, a contradiction in terms; he was the kind of man who did not know the meaning of fear, who shrank from nothing, whose spirits rose highest when things appeared most hopeless. It must, indeed, be an uncommon, even a terrible danger that could shake such nerves; yet Tom saw the signs and read them. Explain to them that he could not, nor did he try. All he knew with certainty was that his brother, sitting now beside him in the cart, hid a secret terror in his heart. Sooner or later, in his own good time, he would share it with him.

He ascribed it, this simple Orkney farmer, to those thirty years of loneliness and exile in wild desolate places, without companionship, without the society of women, with only Indians, husky dogs, a few trappers or fur-dealers like himself, but none of the wholesome, natural influences that sweeten life within reach. Thirty years was a long, long time. He began planning schemes to help. Jim must see people as much as possible, and his mind ran quickly over the men and women available. In women, the neighborhood was not rich, but there were several men of the right sort who might be useful, good fellows all. There was John Rossiter, another old Hudson Bay man, who had been a factor at Cartwright, Labrador, for many years, and had returned long ago to spend his last days in civilization. There was Sandy McKay, also back from a long spell of rubber-planting in Malay... Tom was still busy making plans when they reached the old farm and presently sat down to their first meal together since that early breakfast thirty years ago before Jim caught the steamer that bore him off to exile--an exile that now returned him with nerves unstrung and a secret terror hid in his heart.

"I'll ask no questions," he decided. "Jim will tell me in his own good time. And meanwhile, I'll get him to see as many folks as possible." He meant it too; yet not only for his brother's sake. Jim's terror was so vivid it had touched his own heart too.

"Ah, a man can open his lungs here and breathe!" exclaimed Jim, as the two came out after supper and stood before the house, gazing across the open country. He drew a deep breath as though to prove his assertion, exhaling with slow satisfaction again. "It's good to see a clear horizon and to know there's all that water between--between me and where I've been." He turned his face to watch the plover in the sky, then looked towards the distant shoreline where the sea was just visible in the long evening light. "There can't be too much water for me," he added, half to himself. "I guess they can't cross water--not that much water at any rate."

Tom stared, wondering uneasily what to make of it.

"At the trees again, Jim?" he said laughingly. He had overheard the last words, though spoken low, and thought it best not to ignore them altogether. To be natural was the right way, he believed, natural and cheery. To make a joke of anything unpleasant, he felt, was to make it less serious. "I've never seen a tree come across the Atlantic yet, except as a mast--dead," he added.

"The direct response was, "I wasn't thinking of the trees at that moment but something else. Even though I detest their sight, the wretched trees are nothing. Not much of an issue, but "—as if he was mentally comparing them to something else. He briefly puffs at his pipe.

They can't swim, nor can they move, his brother added.

The notion in Jim's head was undoubted as plain as day, but his voice suddenly became thick but not with smoke, and he spoke incoherently. Things cannot be concealed by them, can they?

Tom laughed, but the expression in his brother's eyes made his laugh as forced-sounding as it was brief, "Not much cover hereabouts, I confess."

"That's so," agreed the other. "But what I meant was"--he threw out his chest, looked about him with an air of intense relief, drew in another deep breath, and again exhaled with satisfaction--"if there are no trees, there's no hiding."

It was the expression on the rugged, weathered face that sent the blood in a sudden gulping rush from his brother's heart. He had seen men frightened, seen men afraid before they were frightened; he had also seen men stiff with terror in the face both of natural and so-called supernatural things; but never in his life before had he seen the look of unearthly dread that now turned his brother's face as white as chalk and yet put the glow of fire in two haunted burning eyes.

Across the darkening landscape, the sound of distant barking had floated to them on the evening wind.

It's only a farm dog barking, I say. However, Jim's low, deep voice was the one who started it while placing one hand on his brother's arm.

"That's it," said Tom, feeling guilty for betraying himself and shocked to see that Jim was suddenly the one providing comfort—a radical shift in their relationship. What did you assume it was, and why?

He made a concerted effort to speak easily and naturally, but his voice trembled. The love and intimacy between the brothers were so intense that they were compelled to share.

Jim dropped his impressive brow. He muttered, "I thought," his grey beard brushing the other's cheek, "maybe it was the wolves," his voice quivering with an agonizing sense of horror, "the Wolves of God!"

II.

The thirty-year difference had been readily crossed; it was the secret, however, that left an unbridged chasm that neither of them desired to fill.

It was possible to speculate as to why Jim hesitated, but Tom's silence presented more of a challenge.

With strong, simple men, strangers to affectation or pretense, the reserve is a real, almost a sacred thing. Jim offered nothing more; Tom asked no single question. In the latter's mind lay, for one thing, a singular intuitive certainty: that if he knew the truth he would lose his brother. How, why, wherefore, he had no notion; whether by death, or because, having told an awful thing, Jim would hide--physically or mentally--he knew not, nor even asked himself. No subtlety lay in Tom, the Orkney farmer. He merely felt that a knowledge of the truth involved separation which was death.

Day and night, however, that extraordinary phrase which, at its first hearing, had frozen his blood, ran on beating in his mind. With it came always the original, nameless horror that had held him motionless where he stood, his brother's bearded lips against his ear: _The Wolves of God_. In some dim way, he sometimes felt--tried to persuade himself, rather--the horror did not belong to the phrase alone, but was a sympathetic echo of what Jim felt himself. It had entered his mind and heart. They had always shared in this same strange, intimate way. The deep brotherly tie accounted for it. Of the possible transference of thought and emotion, he knew nothing, but this was what he meant perhaps.

At the same time he fought and strove to keep it out, not because it brought uneasy and distressing feelings to him, but because he did not wish to pry, to ascertain, to discover his brother's secret as by some kind of subterfuge that seemed too near to eavesdropping almost. Also, he wished most earnestly to protect him. Meanwhile, despite himself, or perhaps because of himself, he watched his brother as a wild animal watches its young. Jim was the only tie he had on earth. He loved him with a brother's love, and Jim, similarly, he knew, loved him. His job was difficult. Love alone could guide him.

He provided opportunities but asked no questions:

"I was surprised by your letter, Jim. I've never felt happier in my entire life.
You still have two more years to serve."

The brief response was, "I'd had enough." God, the dude, returning home was nice!

This, and the blunt talk that followed their first meeting, was all Tom had to go upon, while those eyes that refused to shut watched ceaselessly always. There was an improvement, unless, which never occurred to Tom, it was self-control; there was no more talk of trees and water, the barking of the dogs passed unnoticed, no reference to the loneliness of the backwoods life passed his lips; he spent his days fishing, shooting, helping with the work of the farm, his evenings smoking over a glass--he was more than temperate--and talking over the days of long ago.

The signs of uneasiness still were there, but they were negative, far more suggestive, therefore, than if open and direct. He desired no company, for instance--an unnatural thing, thought Tom, after so many years of loneliness.

It was this and the awkward fact that he had given up two years before his time was finished, renouncing, therefore, a comfortable pension--it was these two big details that stuck with such unkind persistence in his brother's thoughts. Behind both, moreover, ran ever the strange whispered phrase. What the words meant, or whence they were derived, Tom had no possible inkling. Like the wicked refrain of some forbidden song, they haunted him day and night, even his sleep not free from them entirely. All of which, to the simple Orkney farmer, was so new an experience that he knew not how to deal with it at all. Too strong to be flustered, he was at any rate bewildered. And it was for Jim, his brother, he suffered most.

What perplexed him chiefly, however, was the attitude his brother showed towards old John Rossiter. He could almost have imagined that the two men had met and known each other out in Canada, though Rossiter showed him how impossible that was, both in point of time and of geography as well. He had brought them together within the first few days, and Jim, silent, gloomy, morose, even surly, had eyed him like an enemy. Old Rossiter, the milk of human kindness as thick in his veins as cream, had taken no offense. A grizzled veteran of the wilds, he had served his full term with the Company and now enjoyed his well-earned pension. He was full of stories, reminiscences, adventures of every sort and kind; he knew men and values, had seen strange things that only the true wilderness delivers, and he loved nothing better than to tell them over a glass. He talked with Jim so genially and affably that little response was called for luckily, for Jim was glum and unresponsive almost to rudeness. Old Rossiter noticed nothing. What Tom noticed was, chiefly perhaps, his brother's acute uneasiness. Between his desire to help, his attachment to Rossiter, and his keen personal distress, he knew not what to do or say. The situation was becoming too much for him.

What perplexed him chiefly, however, was the attitude his brother showed towards old John Rossiter. He could almost have imagined that the two men had met and known each other out in Canada, though Rossiter showed him how impossible that was, both in point of time and of geography as well. He had brought them together within the first few days, and Jim, silent, gloomy, morose, even surly, had eyed him like an enemy. Old Rossiter, the milk of human kindness as thick in his veins as cream, had taken no offense. A grizzled veteran of the wilds, he had served his full term with the Company and now enjoyed his well-earned pension. He was full of stories, reminiscences, adventures of every sort and kind; he knew men and values, had seen strange things that only the true wilderness delivers, and he loved nothing better than to tell them over a glass. He talked with Jim so genially and affably that little response was called for luckily, for Jim was glum and unresponsive almost to rudeness. Old Rossiter noticed nothing. What Tom noticed was, chiefly perhaps, his brother's acute uneasiness. Between his desire to help, his attachment to Rossiter, and his keen personal distress, he knew not what to do or say. The situation was becoming too much for him.

The two families, besides--Peace and Rossiter--had been neighbors for generations, had intermarried freely, and were related in various degrees. He was too fond of his brother to feel ashamed, but he was glad when the visit was over and they were out of their host's house. Jim had even declined to drink with him.

"On their drive home, Tom remarked, "They're good guys on the island, but maybe not amusing. But we all stick together. They are mainly trustworthy."

Tom received a stern reply that said, "I never was a talker. "You realize that." Tom, who understood more than he did, accepted the apology and gave him a lot of leeways.

He assisted him by saying, "John likes to talk." He values a patient listener.

The response was, "I'm done with that kind of talk." "I'm no longer interested in the Company or what they are doing. It's enough for me."

Tom noticed other things as well with those affectionate eyes of his that did not want to see yet would not close. As the days drew in, for instance, Jim seemed reluctant to leave the house towards evening. Once the full light of day had passed, he kept indoors. He was eager and ready enough to shoot in the early morning, no matter at what hour he had to get up, but he refused point blank to go with his brother to the lake for an evening flight. No excuse was offered; he simply declined to go.

The gap between them thus widened and deepened, while yet in another sense it grew less formidable. Both knew, that is, that a secret lay between them for the first time in their lives, yet both knew also that at the right and proper moment it would be revealed. Jim only waited till the proper moment came. And Tom understood. His deep, simple love was equal to all emergencies. He respected his brother's reserve. The obvious desire of John Rossiter to talk and ask questions, for instance, he resisted staunchly as far as he was able. Only when he could help and protect his brother did he yield a little. The talk was brief, even monosyllabic; neither the old Hudson Bay fellow nor the Orkney farmer ran to many words:

"He ain't right with himself," offered John, taking his pipe out of his mouth and leaning forward. "That's what I don't like to see." He put a skinny hand on Tom's knee and looked earnestly into his face as he said it.

Jim!" the other yelled back. Do you mean Jim Ill? It sounded absurd.

He has a diseased mind.

Tom said, "I don't understand," even though the truth cut the brother's heart like a piece of rough-edged steel.

"Then, if you like that, his soul."

After a little internal struggle, Tom begged him to be more specific.

The elderly backwoodsman said, laconic, "More'n I can say." "I am not sure about myself. Some men are cured by the woods while others become ill."

"Maybe, John, maybe." Tom fought back his resentment. "You've lived, like him, in lonely places. You ought to know." His mouth shut with a snap, as though he had said too much. Loyalty to his suffering brother caught him strongly. Already his heart ached for Jim. He felt angry with Rossiter for his divination, but perceived, too, that the old fellow meant well and was trying to help him. If he lost Jim, he lost the world--his all.

A considerable pause followed, during which both men puffed their pipes with reckless energy. Both, that is, we're a bit excited. Yet both had their code, a code they would not exceed for worlds.

Jim ain't quite up to the mark, I'll grant that, Tom said afterward, trying to meet the sympathy halfway.

Another lengthy pause followed, during which Rossiter maintained steady eye contact with his buddy while maintaining an expressionless expression – a habit the woods had instilled in him.

"Jim is skeered, he murmured slowly and trying. And what frightens him is his soul."

Tom wavered dreadfully then. He saw that old Rossiter, experienced backwoodsman and taught by the Company as he was, knew where the secret lay if he did not yet know its exact terms. It was easy enough to put the question, yet he hesitated because loyalty forbade.

The elderly man said to himself, "It's a nasty outfit somewhere."

Tom quickly stood up. He yelled fiercely, "You're neither my friend nor his if you talk like way." As he said that, his rage increased. He yelled, "If you say it again, I'll knock your teeth out!"

He took a seat, briefly speechless.

"Forgive me, John," he faltered, shamed yet still angry. "It's pain to me, it's pain. Jim," he went on, after a long breath and a pull at his glass, "Jim _is_ scared, I know it." He waited a moment, hunting for the words that he could use without disloyalty. "But it's nothing he's done himself," he said, "nothing to his discredit. I know _that_."

Old Rossiter raised his head, his eyes displaying an odd brightness.

No offense, he whispered.

Tom abruptly sprang back up and exclaimed, "Tell me what you know."

The elderly factor fixed his eyes on him firmly and squarely. He set his pipe down.

Do you truly want to be told? He questioned in a quiet voice. "Because if you don't, please explain why straight away. I've always been for justice, he continued."

"Tell me," said Tom, his heart in his mouth. "Maybe, if I knew--I might help him." The old man's words woke fear in him. He well knew his passionate, remorseless sense of justice.

The other echoed, "Help him. "There is no assistance for a man who is terrified inside. But if you're interested, I'll tell you."

Tell me, Tom cried. Mounting rage pushed back rising terror as he said, "I _will_ help him."

John shook his glass once more.

Just keep it between us, please.

Between us," Tom said. "Go ahead and do it."

The tiny space was completely silent. The wind was behind it and just the sound of the waves entered.

Old Rossiter muttered, "The Wolves. The Wolf of God

Tom sat still in his chair, as though struck in the face. He shivered. He kept silent and the silence seemed to him long and curious. His heart was throbbing, the blood in his veins played strange tricks. All he remembered was that old Rossiter had gone on talking. The voice, however, sounded far away and distant. It was all unreal, he felt, as he went homewards across the bleak, wind-swept upland, the sound of the sea forever in his ears...

Yes, old John Rossiter, damned is his soul, had gone on talking. He had said wild, incredible things. Damned, be his soul! His teeth should be smashed for that. It was outrageous, it was cowardly, it was not true.

"Jim," he thought, "my brother, Jim!" as he plowed his way wearily against the wind. "I'll teach him. I'll teach him to spread such wicked tales!" He referred to Rossiter. "God blast these fellows! They come home from their outlandish places and think they can say anything! I'll knock his yellow dog's teeth...!"

While, inside, his heart went quailing, crying for help, afraid.

He tried hard to remember exactly what old John had said. Round Garden Lake--that's where Jim was located in his lonely Post--there was a tribe of Redskins. They were of an unusual type. Malefactors among them--thieves, criminals, murderers--were not punished. They were merely turned out by the Tribe to die.

But how?

The Wolves of God took care of them. What were the Wolves of God?

A pack of wolves the Redskins held in awe, a sacred pack, a spirit pack--God curse the man! Absurd, outlandish nonsense! Superstitious humbug! A pack of wolves that punished malefactors, killing but never eating them. "Torn but not eaten," the words came back to him, "white men as well as red. They could even cross the sea...."

"He ought to be strung up for telling such wild yarns. By God--I'll teach him!"

"Jim! My brother, Jim! It's monstrous."

But the elderly man had said something even worse in his fervent, cold justice, which Tom would never forget because he could never forgive it: "He must be sent away; you cannot retain him in this area. He cannot stay on the island with us." And for that, even though he could hardly believe what he was hearing, for that, for which the appropriate response was a punch to the lips, Tom realized that his once-close friendship and affection had converted to venomous hatred.

"My God, and Jim, forgive me if I don't kill him for that damned lie!"

III.

A few days later, the islands were hit by the storm, which caused them to quiver in their sea-born bed. Lightning lighted the skies, and there was severe wind tearing over the area devoid of trees. Such rain had never before been observed. The structure trembled and shuddered. The sea almost appeared to have overflowed her bounds as the waves poured in. Both of the brothers were impacted by its rage and the wind's noises, but Jim found the commotion to be the most unpleasant. It made him gloomy, mute, and depressed. Tom saw right away that it made him uneasy. The repulsive phrase, "Scared in his soul," returned to him.

"God saves anyone who's out tonight," said Jim anxiously, as the old farm rattled about his head. Whereupon the door opened as of itself. There was no knock. It flew wide as if the wind had burst it. Two drenched and beaten figures showed in the gap against the lurid sky--old John Rossiter and Sandy. They laid their fowling pieces down and took off their capes; they had been up at the lake for the evening flight and six birds were in the game bag. So suddenly had the storm come up that they had been caught before they could get home.

And, while Tom welcomed them, looked after their creature wants, and made them feel at home as in duty bound, no visit, he felt at the same time, could have been less opportune. Sandy did not matter--Sandy never did matter anywhere, his personality being negligible--but John Rossiter was the last man Tom wished to see just then. He hated the man; hated that sense of implacable justice that he knew was in him; with the slightest excuse he would have turned him out and sent him on to his own home, storm or no storm. But Rossiter provided no excuse; he was all gratitude and easy politeness, more pleasant and friendly to Jim even than to his brother. Tom set out the whisky and sugar, sliced the lemon, put the kettle on, and furnished dry coats while the soaked garments hung up before the roaring fire that Orkney makes customary even when days are warm.

"It might be the equinoctials," observed Sandy, "if it wasn't late October." He shivered, for the tropics had thinned his blood.

"This ain't no ordinary storm," put in Rossiter, drying his drenched boots. "It reminds me a bit"--he jerked his head to the window that gave seawards, the rush of rain against the panes half drowning his voice--"reminds me a bit of yonder." He looked up, as though to find someone to agree with him, only one such person being in the room.

"Sure, it ain't," agreed Jim at once, but speaking slowly, "no ordinary storm." His voice was quiet as a child's. Tom, stooping over the kettle, felt something cold go trickling down his back. "It's from across the Atlantic too."

"All our big storms come from the sea," offered Sandy, saying just what Sandy was expected to say. His lank red hair lay matted on his forehead, making him look like an unhappy collie dog.

"There's no hospitality," Rossiter changed the talk, "like an islander's," as Tom mixed and filled the glasses. "He doesn't even ask 'Say when?'" He chuckled in his beard and turned to Sandy, well pleased with the compliment to his host. "Now, in Malay," he added dryly, "it's probably different, I guess." And the two men, one from Labrador, the other from the tropics, fell to bantering one another with heavy humor, while Tom made things comfortable and Jim stood silent with his back to the fire. At each blow of the wind that shook the building, a suitable remark was made, generally by Sandy: "Did you hear that now?" "Ninety miles an hour at least." "Good thing you build solid in this country!" while Rossiter occasionally repeated that it was an "uncommon storm" and that "it reminded" him of the northern tempests he had known "out yonder."

Tom said little, one thought, and one thought only in his heart--the wish that the storm would abate and his guests depart. He felt uneasy about Jim. He hated Rossiter. In the kitchen he had steadied himself already with a good stiff drink, and was now halfway through a second; the feeling was in him that he would need their help before the evening was out. Jim, he noticed, had left his glass untouched. His attention went to the wind and the outer night; he added little to the conversation.

"Hark!" cried Sandy's shrill voice. "Did you hear that? That wasn't wind, I'll swear." He sat up, looking for all the world like a dog pricking its ears to something no one else could hear.

"The sea coming over the dunes," said Rossiter. "There'll be an awful tide tonight and a terrible sea off the Swarf. Moon at the full, too." He cocked his head sideways to listen. The roaring was tremendous, waves and wind combining with a result that almost shook the ground. Rain hit the glass with incessant volleys like a duck shot.

Jim finally spoke at that point after being silent for a while.

It's wonderful there aren't any trees, he murmured. "That's great," I said.

Sandy remarked, "There'd be awful harm, wouldn't there? They could also fall on the house.

But it was the tone Jim used that made Rossiter turn stiffly in his chair, looking first at the speaker, then at his brother. Tom caught both glances and saw the hard keen glitter in the eyes. This kind of talk, he decided, had got to stop, yet how to stop it he hardly knew, for he was not subtle methods, and rudeness to his guests ran too strong against the island customs. He refilled the glasses, thinking in his blunt fashion about how best to achieve his object when Sandy helped the situation without knowing it.

"That's my first," he observed, and all burst out laughing. For Sandy's tenth glass was equally his "first," and he absorbed his liquor like a sponge, yet showed no effects of it until the moment when he would suddenly collapse and sink helplessly to the ground. The glass in question, however, was only his third, the final moment still far away.

"Three in one and one in three," said Rossiter, amid the general laughter, while Sandy, grave as a judge, half emptied it at a single gulp. Good-natured, obtuse as a cart horse, the tropics, it seemed, had first worn out his nerves, then removed them entirely from his body. "That's Malay theology, I guess," finished Rossiter. And the laugh broke out again. Whereupon, setting his glass down, Sandy offered his usual explanation that the hot lands had thinned his blood, that he felt the cold in these "arctic islands," and that alcohol was a necessity of life with him. Tom, grateful for the unexpected help, encouraged him to talk, and Sandy, accustomed to neglect, as a rule, responded readily. Having saved the situation, however, he now unwittingly led it back into the danger zone.

"A night for tales, eh?" he remarked, as the wind came howling with a burst of strangest noises against the house.

"Down there in the States," he went on, "they'd say the evil spirits were out. They're a superstitious crowd, the natives. I remember once----" And he told a tale, half foolish, half interesting, of a mysterious track he had seen when the following buffalo in the jungle. It ran close to the spoor of a wounded buffalo for miles, a track unlike that of any known animal, and the natives, though unable to name it, regarded it with awe. It was a good sign, a kill was certain. They said it was a spirit track.

"You got your buffalo?" asked Tom.

"Found him two miles away, lying dead. The mysterious spoor came to an end close beside the carcass. It didn't continue."

"And that reminds me----" began old Rossiter, ignoring Tom's attempt to introduce another subject. He told them of the haunted island at Eagle River and a tale of the man who would not stay buried on another island off the coast. From that he went on to describe the strange man-beast that hides in the deep forests of Labrador, manifesting but rarely, and dangerous to men who stray too far from camp, men with a passion for wildlife over-strong in their blood--the great mythical Wendigo. And while he talked, Tom noticed that Sandy used each pause as a good moment for a drink, but that Jim's glass remained untouched.

The atmosphere of incredible things, thus, grew in the little room, much as it gathers among the shadows around a forest camp-fire when men who have seen strange places of the world give tongue about them, knowing they will not be laughed at--an atmosphere, once established, it is vain to fight against. The ingrained superstition that hides in every mother's son comes up at such times to breathe. It came up now. Sandy, closer by several glasses to the moment, Tom saw, when he would be suddenly drunk, gave birth again, a tale this time of a Scottish planter who had brutally dismissed a native servant for no other reason than that he disliked him. The man disappeared completely, but the villagers hinted that he would--soon indeed that he had--come back, though "not quite as he went." The planter was armed, knowing that vengeance might be violent. A black panther, meanwhile, was seen prowling about the bungalow. One night noise outside his door on the veranda roused him. Just in time to see the black brute leaping over the railings into the compound, he fired, and the beast fell with a savage growl of pain. Help arrived and more shots were fired into the animal, as it lay, mortally wounded already, lashing its tail upon the grass. The lanterns, however, showed that instead of a panther, it was the servant they had shot to shreds.

Sandy told the story well, a certain odd conviction in his tone and manner, neither of them at all to the liking of his host. Uneasiness and annoyance had been growing in Tom for some time already, his inability to control the situation adding to his anger. Emotion was accumulating in him dangerously; it was directed chiefly against Rossiter, who, though saying nothing definite, somehow deliberately encouraged both talk and atmosphere. Given the conditions, it was natural enough that the talk should take the turn it did take, but what made Tom angrier and angrier was that, if Rossiter had not been present, he could have stopped it easily enough. It was the presence of the old Hudson Bay man that prevented his taking decided action. He was afraid of Rossiter, afraid of putting his back up. That was the truth. His recognition of it made him furious.

"Tell us another, Sandy McKay," said the veteran. "There's a lot in such tales. They're found the world over--men turning into animals and the like."

And Sandy, yet nearer to his moment of collapse, but still showing no effects, obeyed willingly. He noticed nothing; the whisky was good, his tales were appreciated, and that sufficed him. He thanked Tom, who just then refilled his glass, and went on with his tale. But Tom, hatred, and fury in his heart, had reached the point where he could no longer contain himself, and Rossiter's last words inflamed him. He went over, under cover of a tremendous clap of wind, to fill the old man's glass. The latter refused, covering the tumbler with his big, lean hand. Tom stood over him a moment, lowering his face. "You keep still," he whispered ferociously, but so that no one else heard it. He glared into his eyes with an intensity that held danger, and Rossiter, without answering, flung back that glare with equal, but with a calmer, anger.

In the meantime, the wind played a joke by deviating, and each time it did, Jim's seat moved as well. He seemed to prefer facing the sound to turning away from it.

After Sandy had finished, Rossiter replied, "Your chance now for a tale." Jim was repositioning his chair when he noticed him looking across at him after hearing the gust of wind hit the walls behind him.

The onslaught also rattled the windows and door facing him. Without responding, Jim stood motionless as death for a brief period before making a decision.

Rossiter observed, "It's beating up from all sides like it was going around the structure.

There was a moment's pause, the four men listening with awe to the roar and power of the terrific wind. Tom listened too, but at the same time watched, wondering vaguely why he didn't cross the room and crash his fist into the old man's chattering mouth. Jim put out his hand and took his glass, but did not raise it to his lips. And a lull came abruptly in the storm, the wind sinking into a moment's dreadful silence. Tom and Rossiter turned their heads in the same instant and stared into each other's eyes. For Tom, the instant seemed enormously prolonged. He realized the challenge in the other and that his rudeness had roused it into action. It had become a contest of wills--Justice battling against Love.

Jim's glass had now reached his lips, and the chattering of his teeth against its rim was audible.

But the lull passed quickly and the wind began again, though so gently at first, it had the sound of innumerable swift footsteps treading lightly, of countless hands fingering the doors and windows, but then suddenly with a mighty shout as it swept against the walls, rushed across the roof and descended like a battering-ram against the farther side.

"God, did you hear that?" cried Sandy. "It's trying to get in!" and having said it, he sank in a heap beside his chair, all of a sudden completely drunk. "It's wolves or panthers," he mumbled in his stupor on the floor, "but what she's happened to Malay?" It was the last thing he said before unconsciousness took him, and apparently, he was insensible to the kick on the head from a heavy farmer's boot. For Jim's glass had fallen with a crash and the second kick was stopped midway. Tom stood spell-bound, unable to move or speak, as he watched his brother suddenly cross the room and open a window into the very teeth of the gale.

"Let be! Let be!" came the voice of Rossiter, an authority in it, a curious gentleness too, both of them new. He had risen, his lips were still moving, but the words that issued from them were inaudible, as the wind and rain leaped with galloping violence into the room, smashing the glass to atoms and dashing a dozen loose objects helter-skelter onto the floor.

"I saw it!" cried Jim, in a voice that rose above the din and clamor of the elements. He turned and faced the others, but it was at Rossiter he looked. "I saw the leader." He shouted to make himself heard, although the tone was quiet. "A splash of white on his great chest. I saw them all!"

At the words, and the expression in Jim's eyes, old Rossiter, white to the lips, dropped back into his chair as if a blow had struck him. Tom, petrified, felt his heart stop. For through the broken window, above yet within the wind, came the sound of a wolf-pack running, howling in deep, full-throated chorus, mad for blood. It passed like a whirlwind and was gone. And, of the three men so close together, one sitting and two standing, Jim alone was in that terrible moment wholly master of himself.

He turned and stared directly into each person's eyes one after another before the others could talk or move. His speech recalled his time spent in the wilderness:

I did it," he murmured reassuringly. I murdered him, and I was able to leave.

He took one step, threw open the door, and disappeared into the shadows with a face painted with a look of mystical dread.

So quick were both words and action, that Tom's paralysis passed only as the draught from the broken window banged the door behind him. He seemed to leap across the room, old Rossiter, tears on his cheeks and his lips mumbling foolish words, so close upon his heels that the backward blow of fury Tom aimed at his face caught him only in the neck and sent him reeling sideways to the floor instead of flat upon his back.

"Murderer! My brother's death upon you!" he shouted as he tore the door open again and plunged out into the night.

And the odd thing that happened then, the thing that touched old John Rossiter's reason, leaving him from that moment till his death a foolish man of uncertain mind and memory, happened when he and the unconscious, drink-sodden Sandy lay alone together on the stone floor of that farm-house room.

Rossiter, dazed by the blow and his fall, but in full possession of his senses, and the anger gone out of him owing to what he had brought about, this same John Rossiter sat up and saw Sandy also sitting up and staring at him hard. And Sandy was sober as a judge, his eyes and speech both clear, even his face unflushed.

"John Rossiter," he said, "it was not God who appointed you executioner. It was the devil." And his eyes, thought Rossiter, were like the eyes of an angel.

He gasped, "Sandy McKay," his breath slipping away as his teeth chattered. Sandra McKay! It was the only phrase he could think of. But Sandy was already back in his coma and had collapsed intoxicated and helpless on the floor of the farm home. He stayed there until daybreak.

Despite the most thorough searches, Jim's remains were buried amid the sand for several months. It was exposed by yet another storm. It was covered in sand. The clothing was gone, leaving the tattered but uneaten body exposed to the wind and sun of December.

9 798887 728421

Printed by Libri Plureos GmbH in Hamburg, Germany